MAG...

Ge...

Pirate
Adventure

Written by Kate Cary
Illustrated by Rob Chapman

HENDERSON
PUBLISHING LTD

©1997 HENDERSON PUBLISHING LTD

Contents

1. An Old Sea Dog's Errand

Gemma was sitting cross-legged on her bed. A reading lamp, clipped to her bedpost, pointed in her direction. It spotlighted the small patch of duvet where she was sitting. In the corners of her room, bedtime shadows danced in the early evening light.

On her right knee, Gemma balanced a glass of orange juice, cupping her hand around it to stop it toppling off. On her left knee, a tattered book lay open, its covers flapping backwards, and its jacket dangling down on either side. She pinned it to her knee with two fingers as she read.

Down the hall, she could faintly hear her brother, Simon, tootling on another of the weird instruments he had brought home from school. Otherwise, the house was quiet. Dad was, no doubt, sorting through his baseball card collection. Mum was probably reading the paper, and Katie was rehearsing her lines for the school play.

"Peace and quiet," sighed Gemma, but she didn't entirely approve. She let the book tumble off her knee and reached for her Walkman. Expertly, she snapped the headphones around her head with one hand, and clicked the play button. She dragged her book back on to her knee, leaving the crumpled jacket behind on the duvet, and began to search the next chapter for pictures. She had no idea that someone was stomping down the hallway towards her door.

"Ah ha! Jim lad!"

Gemma almost spilled her juice when her sister burst into the bedroom.

"Land ahoy, Cap'n!" bellowed Katie, as she flung the door wide and switched on Gemma's bedroom light. She waved a cardboard cutlass above her head and shouted "Shiver me timmmm-berrrrs!" in the gruffest voice she could muster.

Gemma put her glass down on her bedside table. She dragged the head-phones from her ears and looked at her little sister.

Katie was dressed in a blue and white

striped T-shirt and a pair of cut-off jeans that reached down to her knees. Below, two long socks (boldly striped in red and white) hugged her skinny legs. Her tiny feet were swamped in an oversized pair of shiny black shoes, decorated with huge stuck-on buckles that had been cut out of cardboard and painted silver. Katie was grinning. She had used Mum's eyeliner to draw a long black moustache under her nose, and she had tied a red spotty scarf around her head, fixing it at the back with a big knot under her thick plait.

"Well, what do you think then?" Mum appeared in the doorway behind Katie. "Does she look like a scurvy sea dog?" she asked.

Katie was going to play a pirate in the school Christmas play. They were staging *Treasure Island* this year.

"Wow!" replied Gemma. She was impressed with Katie's transformation. "All she needs now is an earring – a big, golden hoop dangling from one ear."

"You're right," agreed Mum.

"I think I've got just the thing she needs

in my jewellery box," said Gemma. She clambered off her bed and stepped carefully around the books and clothes which littered her bedroom floor. Mum and Katie waited as Gemma scrabbled under her bed for her jewellery box.

"I bet real pirates never used to say 'shiver me timbers'," said Gemma, as she lifted the small wooden box out on to her dressing table.

"They did so!" retorted Katie indignantly. "Mrs Bothwell said so."

"And how many pirates does Mrs Bothwell know?" teased Gemma, opening the lid.

"As many as you do!" huffed Katie.

"Ah, here it is," announced Gemma, holding up a golden hoop earring which she had dug out from the bottom. "I can't see the matching one, but you only want one, don't you?" Bracelets and necklaces spilled out on to her dressing table.

"That's perfect," said Mum, reaching for the earring. "Come on Katie, let's go and try it on. Thank you, Gemma."

Mum and Katie turned and headed back

up the hall, closing the door behind them. Gemma began to scoop the pile of glittering beads and bangles back into her jewellery box. Right at the bottom of the shimmering heap, she spotted the matching earring, hooked on to a necklace. Delicately, she untangled it and held it to one ear. She looked up into the dusty, wooden-framed mirror that sat on her dressing table and tried out Katie's words, half-whispering, "Ah ha! Jim lad!"

In her jeans and sweatshirt, Gemma decided that she didn't look much like a bloodthirsty pirate. Pirates didn't usually have pale skin, soft eyes or button noses. With her fair hair, half-scrunched into the remains of a school plait, she looked far more like Jim Hawkins, the young cabin boy in Katie's school play. Gemma pulled up a chair and sat down, still looking in the mirror.

I suppose cabin boy is better than nothing, she decided. She fastened the earring to her ear and began sifting once more through her jewellery box. For a moment, she imagined that she was really feeling the cold, sharp edges of priceless jewels running through her fingers. She lifted out a handful of beads and shook loose the bangles and earrings that were tangled around them.

There, in her fingers, Gemma held a simple black and white necklace. It felt heavy in her hand. It was beautiful. The white beads shone with a depth she had seen in the pearls her mother wore on special occasions; they might have been plucked from the Indian Ocean itself. The ebony stones could easily have been carried from the China Seas in the ship of a Spanish adventurer. This was one of the necklaces which she had found on the beach in Cornwall – one of her special necklaces, which brought adventure and excitement. Gemma held the necklace to her throat.

"I fancy this flashy trinket will fetch us an adventure or two," she said to her reflection, mimicking the rich, rolling accent of a Cornish fisherman. She undid the clasp, draped the beads around her neck and fastened them on behind. As she did so, she could hear a voice in her head, chanting,

You shall journey far and wide
Across Time's endless seas...

And as the voice chanted, Gemma felt herself falling down, down, down, down...

Half a second later, the falling sensation stopped, and Gemma found that instead of smooth, warm wood, she could feel the sandy rasp of stone beneath her fingertips.

She opened her eyes. The subdued electric light of her bedroom had been transformed into bright and unclouded daylight. The jewellery box had disappeared and instead, crystal water glinted before her, sparkling aquamarine in the sunshine. Straight ahead, instead of a dressing table mirror, a sapphire sky met a turquoise sea as a smooth and distant horizon.

Gemma was no longer at home in her cosy bedroom. She was sitting on the side of a harbour, perched on the edge of a wall. Her feet were dangling down towards clear, blue water. Tall ships swayed in front of her on gently swelling waves; their huge hulls sitting high in the water, their sails rolled neatly away, their towering masts laced with ropes.

The familiar smell of fresh sea air filled Gemma with a tingling sense of belonging. How many times had she stood on the harbour side with her uncle in Cornwall and watched the fishing boats come and go? Slowly, calmly, so that she did not draw attention to herself, Gemma looked around.

The harbour lay in a tiny cove. Its rocky cliffs were topped with the greenest vegetation Gemma had ever seen. Palm trees leaned against the smooth blue sky, tropical grasses grew tall and thick around them, and large bushes dotted the hillsides.

Peering over her shoulder, Gemma saw a crowd of ramshackle houses. A small town was squeezed in between the cliffs and the sea. Its buildings were brightly painted – blue, yellow, pink and green. They glowed brilliantly in the sunlight.

The quayside was thronging with people, as bright and colourful as the houses. Men were dressed in fine shirts with frilled collars and long, baggy trousers, or short, tight breeches and shiny silk stockings up to their knees. There were women with hair piled high on top of their heads. They wore bright, full skirts with low hems that dragged in the dust. A few had tied big knots in the side, to hitch them up out of the dirt, or they had tucked their hem into their waistband, showing a flash of ribboned bloomer every now and then. They wore vivid corsets, laced tightly around their waists, and splendid, voluminous blouses that fluttered in the sea breeze.

Suddenly, Gemma was shaken by a harsh, loud voice below her.

"Boy! Boy! Here! D'you want to earn yourself a penny?" Gemma looked down.

"Hey, you there!" A wiry, wrinkled man, with a grey beard and wild white hair, was balancing in a rowing boat beneath her feet.

"Yes, you!" he shouted impatiently, waving one hand wildly at Gemma, "Boy!"

The wooden boat was bobbing on the waves, nudging against the harbour wall. The old man was having difficulty trying to stand, wave and shout all at the same time, without toppling overboard.

"What, me? Do you mean me?" called Gemma.

"Who else would I mean?" bellowed the man in a voice as rough as sea salt. "Screamin' Spaniards! Where's you from? You sounds even stranger than you looks, boy. Did them Quakers leave you behind?" He didn't wait for an answer. "Tell them they's wasting their time here; Port Calico is no place for good, Christian folk!"

"I'm not a bo..." began Gemma, but the old man wasn't interested in listening. He had managed to get a firm grip on an iron ring which jutted out halfway up the harbour wall, and he was finding it easier to balance as his boat rose and fell on the waves beneath him.

"But I expect a young lad like yourself would like to earn a penny – Quaker or not," he croaked loudly. "Them who's not greedy for money in the Caribbean are fools, and you wouldn't want me thinkin' you's a fool, lad, for I don't suffer fools gladly." The old man narrowed his eyes. Gemma suddenly noticed how icy blue they were.

"Run up to Drake's Drum, fast as you can," he began, "and tell Scrimp that the tide's on the turn and the *Good Fortune* is weighing anchor and about to set sail."

"Who's Scrimp?" asked Gemma.

"The innkeeper, you brainless eel!" snapped the old man.

Gemma looked down. She was no longer sure whether this elderly sailor was asking her or ordering her to go. She thought that she could see the round wooden handle and shiny metal trigger of a pistol sticking out of his waistcoat pocket. Nervously, she asked, "But – what's Drake's Drum?"

"You must be very new to Turtle Island," replied the old man. His eyes suddenly crinkled with cold pleasure, as if he had just found the last toffee in a bag full of empty sweet wrappers. His voice softened into a mocking whine. "Why, it's a tavern, just up Swordfish Street, starboard, beside Henry Flintlock's workshop." Gemma looked bewildered. The old man began again.

"Find Flintlock's workshop – there's a sign outside, shaped like a blunderbuss. Take the street that runs up beside it, on the starboard side. Then take the first side street you comes to, starboard again, up Marlin Lane, past Pegleg's woodwork shop, and you'll see the tavern, opposite the Stuck Pig. Don't go into the Stuck Pig by mistake, though; you're likely to get your head blown off in that partic'lar tavern, and I need you in one piece to deliver my message. You'll get your penny if you return."

"But, what...?" tried Gemma.

"Be off, you scrawny shrimp!" cursed the old man, his tone turning mean once more, "the tide don't wait for dawdlers nor devilfish!"

Gemma stood up and stepped back from the edge of the harbour wall until the old man was out of sight. She had no wish to make an enemy of this fellow in case she bumped into him again – she suspected that he was not a forgiving man. Even now, she could hear him shouting from his boat,

"Stop shillyshallying, Quaker boy!"

Quickly, Gemma scanned the harbour front for a blunderbuss-shaped sign. Something told her that this was not going to be easy. For a start, she had absolutely no idea what a blunderbuss looked like.

2. Drake's Drum Tavern

"Excuse me," piped Gemma. She tweaked the dangling sleeve of the woman beside her.

"What?" snapped the woman, peering down at Gemma. Gemma hesitated, unnerved by the woman's gruff tone.

"What?" snarled the woman impatiently.

"Can you tell me which one is Henry Flintlock's workshop, please?" she asked. The woman snorted and pointed across the dock towards a higgledy-piggledy line of shop fronts and houses.

"Thank you," said Gemma, and weaved her way through the crowd towards the row of buildings.

There was only one shop with a street running along beside it. Outside dangled a sign shaped like a big, fat pistol, with a nozzle like a trumpet. That must be a blunderbuss, decided Gemma. She marched past the shop and up the narrow street.

It was chilly out of the sunshine, and the dusty dirt beneath her feet was patched with moss. Gemma was happy to take the first right turn she came to. It led into a wider, sunnier street lined with colourful houses. As she passed, she noticed that the buildings were tatty and dilapidated, with broken shutters and shingles missing from the roofs, and front doors hanging half off their hinges. Faded signs dangled unevenly from most of the crumbling half-timbered buildings, riddled with bullet holes and painted with badly spelt words, like Cut-throte Jak's, The Joly Rodger and The Spanyard's Doome. This whole place is filled with taverns, thought Gemma. She stood, looking up at the signs, and swayed dizzily backwards as she wondered where on earth she was and where she was meant to be going. Then she felt something soft and lumpy under her heel, and heard a terrible roar of pain and rage from behind her.

She spun around quickly and found herself staring at the largest silver belt buckle she had ever seen. It sat on the front of a buttoned satin waistcoat which stretched across a wide belly. On either side of the belly lay a richly trimmed coat, slitted with buttonholes and embroidered with silk. Gemma looked up and saw a large, glaring face looming over her. It was almost purple, and close to puffing steam. Long black hair cascaded down around it in neat ringlets, draping itself over two wide shoulders. On the top sat a large, three-cornered hat like one that Dick Turpin might have worn, only bigger and blacker, and with an explosion of feathers and lace shooting out of one side.

Gemma was only half-aware of this fancy rigging; she was concentrating on one thing and one thing alone. She was looking straight into the darkest, reddest, meanest eye that she had ever seen in her life. It might have been forged in a furnace and melted down from red-hot pokers... and right now she felt as though it was burning a hole right through her. She was grateful that there was just one eye. The place where the other should have been was covered by a purple satin patch.

"Watch where you're going, you simpering sprat! I'll have ye keelhauled, yer lubberin' son of a sailor's bunion! I'll feed you to the sharks, I'll, I'll..." Gemma was nearly knocked sideways by the blast of his voice.

"I'm s-s-ssor..." she stammered, trembling.

"You slithering squid! I'll feed your liver to the gulls, I'll..." The pirate put his hand threateningly on the hilt of his cutlass.

"Now, now, Cap'n," said a smooth, syrupy voice from behind him. "We've business to attend to; there's no time for this. He's just a boy – why don't you let him off this time?"

From behind the well-trimmed captain stepped a scruffy-looking man whom Gemma had not noticed before. He was an unlikely saviour; his face was leathery, his nose was squashed, his beard was patchy and only half-grown. His dark, lanky hair was long and tied at the back, and around his neck he wore a dirty blue neckerchief. Beneath it, Gemma could just see a long, fiery scar running from ear to ear. His honey voice dripped unnaturally from a cracked and twisted mouth.

"Say you're sorry to Cap'n Red Eye," he said to Gemma, and smiled up at the captain with a leer that stretched his lips but hardly moved the rest of his face. Gemma could see a brilliant gold tooth shining through the thin gap in his grimace.

"I'm s-s-sorry, Captain Red Eye," she stuttered, taking a deep breath and trying to sound fearless and sorry at the same time. Captain Red Eye scowled down at her, but his hand dropped away from his sword.

"Aye, I suppose so," he growled. "Just

stay out of my way in future, and you might just live to become a real pirate some day." Then, without further ado, he pushed past Gemma and stormed off up the hill, his oily, gold-toothed companion hot on his heels.

"You should be careful of that Cap'n Red Eye," panted a voice behind her. "He eats two young'uns like you every morning for breakfast; he dips 'em in his boiled egg and bites off their heads."

Gemma took a moment to recover herself and another to decide if this new voice was actually speaking to her. She turned to see two green eyes twinkling at her and two round, red cheeks bobbing at the ends of a wide, amiable grin. They belonged to a short, fat sailor. He halted his steady trudge up the steep hill.

"You looks lost, young man," he said kindly.

"I am not a young man!" snapped Gemma, cross at being thought a boy by everyone she met.

"Is that right?" replied the sailor, raising a disbelieving eyebrow. "Don't tell me –

you're as old as Columbus and skipper of your own ship."

"I'm not a young man – I'm a girl!"

"Well tie me up with a sheepshank and feed me to the sharks!" exclaimed the sailor, staring at Gemma's plain grey sweatshirt and faded blue jeans. "Why are you dressed up as a boy? Are you on the run, or do they dress girls in breeches and boys in frilly dresses where you come from?"

"People wear what they like where I come from," said Gemma pompously.

"You must be a funny-looking bunch in that case, I reckon. But each to his own. We don't 'ave any laws in Port Calico, 'cept pirate laws, and they says nothing about clothes as far as I know. You can dress how you want, I s'pose, but only Saint Cuthbert knows why a girl'd want to dress like that." Gemma looked down at her favourite sweatshirt, a little offended. The sailor continued.

"What's your name, littl'un, and what are you doing in this part of town? What are you doing in Port Calico at all?

There's pirates even who won't come near this place – they's too fond of their purses and their lives."

"I'm Gemma," said Gemma. "I'm looking for Drake's Drum. I have a message for Scrimp."

"Well, shiver me timbers! I'm Spouter, quartermaster on board the *Sea Princess*. I'm heading that way myself. Why don't you fall in with me and we can go there together."

Gemma was more than happy to fall in with him. No one else in this place had given her so much as a smile since she had arrived, and she felt that she could trust him. There was something about the way he smiled through his ginger beard, and the way his green, spotted scarf sat a little crookedly on his head that reassured her.

"Thank you," she smiled, "that would be great."

Spouter set off up the steep street, and Gemma trotted along beside him.

"Just what does a young landlubber like you have to tell a mean old sea dog like Scrimp Cuttlejack?" puffed Spouter as they climbed.

"I have a message from a sailor down in the harbour," replied Gemma. "He said to tell Scrimp that the *Good Fortune* is weighing anchor and is about to set sail."

"Oh, is she now," said Spouter, looking thoughtful. "There must be a Spanish ship nearby, loaded with gold and jewels from the Main. She'll be scuttlin' home as fast as the wind'll carry her. I hear the cap'n of the *Good Fortune* won't set sail for anything less than a well-laden Portuguese merchantman these days. Those hulks are easy to catch and he's getting lazy now he's made his fortune. You could outrun one of them fat, windjammin' tubs in a half-rigged brigantine."

"Is the *Good Fortune* a pirate ship?" asked Gemma.

"They's all pirate ships in Port Calico. No other ship would dare sail into the harbour."

"Then your ship, the *Sea Princess*, must be a pirate ship too," concluded Gemma. Excitement was beginning to fizz inside her, as she gradually realised that she had arrived slap, bang, right in the middle of a pirate's den.

"Why, of course, but not like the *Good Fortune*. Cap'n Jake Thackery – "

"Is that your captain?" interrupted Gemma.

"Why, he's the only cap'n I'd throw my lot in with. He's the finest sailor in the Caribbean. He might raid a treasure ship or two, but never an English'un. This peace won't last long, and when them two-faced Spaniards start makin' bother, Jake'll be first to the fight. When trouble's brewin', the gov'nor of Turtle Island sets great store by Jake Thackery."

Spouter came to a halt outside a battered-looking building at the top of the steep lane. Every small, square pane of glass in every chipped and splintered window frame was broken. Here, there and everywhere, plaster flaked off the walls. There was no front door at all, and inside Gemma could see a long, low room, filled with broken chairs, upturned tables and a rabble of disorderly pirates. There was no sign of the counter through the rabble, nor any innkeeper. Gemma paused.

"How'd you like me to pass on that message for you?" asked Spouter, eyeing Gemma as she peered nervously into the tavern. "Scrimp might not take too kindly to having girls hanging around his bar – even girls dressed like boys. It might ruin his nasty reputation." Gemma smiled gratefully at Spouter and nodded.

She pressed herself against the crumbling wall of Drake's Drum and peeped in through the doorway. She watched Spouter push his way into the crowd, carefully weaving and dodging to avoid the swaggering pirates who reeled about the room, until he disappeared from view.

Suddenly, a great roar of anger rose from the middle of the commotion and silenced the hubbub. The roar had a familiar ring to it. As the crowd backed away, Gemma saw Captain Red Eye standing puffed out and towering in the middle of the room. His single red eye glittered like a ruby. His left arm was outstretched, and in his hand he held a cutlass. It reached almost a yard – curved, shining and razor sharp – and the tip rested on the throat of a tall, handsome buccaneer. He was dressed in black from head to toe – velvet shirt, taffeta breeches and boots that reached over his knees.

"You stole my gold!" roared Captain Red Eye.

"It wasn't your gold; it was there for the taking, and I got there first," said the buccaneer calmly.

"Everyone knows that when Captain Red Eye says something is his, then it belongs to Captain Red Eye," roared Captain Red Eye even more loudly.

"And everyone knows that by pirate law, taking is owning, and saying is just talking. I took the gold, so I own the gold. And you are all talk!" The buccaneer's soft, deep voice did not quaver, nor did he flinch as Red Eye growled and poked a little harder with his cutlass.

"No one steals my gold and gets away with it," threatened Red Eye.

"Now, now, gentlemen." A third voice

rang out from the encircling crowd. Gemma watched as Spouter stepped out into the middle.

"We's all pirates here, there's no need for fighting each other. There's plenty of gold on the Spanish Main, enough for wily pirates, at least, and you two gentlemen are the wiliest pirates I know. Only halibut-brained filibusters, who don't know their rigging from their rum ration, need fight each other for gold hereabouts. Come now gentlemen, let's not have a kerfuffle."

Captain Red Eye grunted angrily, but reluctantly lowered his cutlass. The buccaneer rubbed his throat with a slender, sunburned hand, then he grinned broadly.

"You caught me unawares, Mr Red Eye," he said, with a twinkle in his eye.

"Well here's a warning," scowled Red Eye nastily, "so's next time you'll know I'm coming. No one crosses Red Eye and gets away with it. Sleep with one eye open from now on, Captain Jake Thackery, 'cause, by the beard of Neptune, I shall be avenged on you!"

So saying, Red Eye turned on his heel and strode towards the doorway. Gemma ducked out of the way just in time as he marched past her. She watched as he stomped away down the street.

Inside the tavern, an oily-looking man with a gold tooth leaned back calmly in his chair and watched the doorway through narrowed eyes. Around him, the crowd of pirates resumed their drinking, laughing and singing.

Spouter pushed his way through to the bar and shouted into the ear of the innkeeper. Scrimp nodded and reached out to ring a large brass bell behind the counter. He bellowed the name of the *Good Fortune* so loud that it could be heard over the noise of the tavern, and right the way down the street. Immediately, pirates began swarming towards the doorway and pushing their way through it. They streamed out of Drake's Drum and galloped unsteadily down the steep road towards the harbour.

The rabble almost knocked Gemma off her feet. By the time she had recovered her balance, and peeped inside the tavern once more, Spouter was sitting at a table with the handsome buccaneer. He spotted Gemma's face in the doorway and beckoned her to come in. Gemma looked around. The bar was almost empty now, except for a handful of men dotted here and there around the room. Scrimp was busy carrying trays full of greasy, pirate-pawed tankards through a low wooden doorway at the back of the bar.

She walked in.

"Well, well, Spouter – have you found me a new cabin boy already?" asked the buccaneer, smiling, as Gemma approached the table.

"This is Gemma," said Spouter. "She comes from a place where they dresses girls as boys and boys as girls."

"Everyone dresses themselves," objected Gemma indignantly, "and we simply dress how we like!"

"Gemma," interrupted Spouter, "meet Jake Thackery, fine Cap'n of the *Sea Princess*." He added to Jake, "I get the feeling that Gemma is new in town. I found her treading on Cap'n Red Eye's toes."

"She sounds like my kind of newcomer," said Jake. Then he asked, "Spouter, where do you find all these waifs and strays? We already have the strangest-looking crew in the Caribbean! What with Will Halfnose, Thomas Twelvefingers and Bald Peg, I suppose you want me to sign this one up as a member of the company as well?"

"Well, it mightn't be such a bad idea," wheedled Spouter. "After all, as you say, we do need a new cabin boy, since Johnny Pugh got himself run through in the Stuck Pig last week. The tide's on the turn and there won't be time to find another before we sail. There's no harm in trying her out. If she don't make the grade, we can always throw her to the sharks." He smiled warmly as he added this, but Gemma didn't hear; she was too busy wondering if she really wanted to join the crew of a pirate ship.

"Well, what do you think?" asked Jake, looking straight at Gemma. "Fancy a life as a pirate?"

The only other thing to do was to stay in Port Calico, but after meeting some of its inhabitants, Gemma did not fancy hanging around. Spouter and Captain Jake seemed to be the nicest people that she had met so far. She made up her mind.

"Yes," she said.

"You'll have to sign the ship's articles and pledge allegiance to your captain and to England."

"Okay," said Gemma confidently.

Jake nodded and stood up.

"Very well. Everyone back to the *Sea Princess*. We set sail at once."

The sailors at the bar drained their tankards, and headed towards the doorway. Jake, Spouter and Gemma followed. Gemma felt her knees tremble slightly as she stepped out of the tavern. She had only been in town for one hour and already she was marching down to the harbour to join a pirate crew and set sail on the high seas.

3. Hatching a Plan

When night fell in Port Calico, the rowdy, staggering crowds which littered the streets in the morning and jammed the harbour side after lunch, went home and fetched their friends. Little did Gemma know, as she rocked gently on a calm, moonlit ocean, just a few miles from the shore, that after dark, Port Calico was reputedly the most vile and unruly port in the Caribbean!

The *Black Heart*, Captain Red Eye's creaking ship, slumbered on the deep, black water of the harbour. The shouts, screams and gunfire explosions from the waterfront could only just be heard inside the captain's shadowy cabin. The light of a hundred taverns strained through the dirty cabin windows. On a rough wooden table, a greasy oil lamp gave out a half-hearted flame that barely lit the narrow room. Captain Red Eye leaned forward in his chair.

"I've spoken to my partner," he said. "He'll know what to do – he's just waiting for the final signal." Red Eye raised his bushy black eyebrows.

The man sitting opposite him took off a black leather glove and reached inside his thick jacket. He drew out a blood-red velvet pouch tied at the top with string. It made a clinking sound as he deposited it on the table.

"Here," he declared. Although only a single word, the man's genteel accent was unmistakable. Anyone who had seen his lace cravat and satin breeches – all the rage in London this year – would have known instantly that this was a gentleman straight from the English royal court.

Red Eye picked up the velvet bag from the table and tipped out a handful of gold coins.

"There'll be a thousand doubloons more when you give me the letter," said the Englishman.

Red Eye leaned back in his chair. He felt very pleased with himself. It had taken all his willpower not to kill Jake Thackery as he stood beaming in Drake's Drum that morning, but he had resisted, and now it was paying off. Thackery was alive and well and ready to fall into the trap that Red Eye had set for him. It would be a pleasure to get rid of that handsome sea serpent, once and for all, and pay him back for all the times he had stolen treasure from under the nose of Captain Red Eye. He smiled wryly. This revenge was going to be sweet, he thought, weighing the coins in his palm – and profitable as well.

"So," he said, in a matter-of-fact way, "you want me to steal a letter from Jake Thackery's ship."

"Yes. His official permission to raid Spanish ships and ports, signed by the governor of Turtle Island."

Captain Red Eye gasped, as if he'd never plundered a ship in his life. "But England's at peace with Spain these days. We can't be raidin' their ships any more."

"Precisely. If it were known at court that the governor was still encouraging Captain Thackery's anti-Spanish activities, he would be relieved of his duties." The

Englishman watched Red Eye slyly. "And Captain Thackery would find himself dangling at the end of a rope on Executioner's Dock before the year was out."

The pirate captain's crimson eye twinkled at the thought. Then he asked suspiciously, "What d'you care what the governor does? I can't believe an Englishman wants to defend them greedy Spaniards."

"I have a friend who is keen to become the new governor of Turtle Island. He hears that it's a profitable post. And," he added, "I expect he would be *very* grateful to any man who had helped him obtain it."

"Is that so?"

"I'd say that, with a well-disposed governor and without Captain Thackery, the seas around Turtle Island – and the ships that sail in them – would be yours for the taking. All you have to do is find that letter and hand it over to me."

Aboard the *Sea Princess*, Gemma was rocking gently on a moonlit ocean, but she was not asleep. After introducing her to the rest of the crew, Jake had set Gemma to work in his cabin, shining up the lanterns, dusting down the furniture and polishing the windows.

"When everything shines like Sir Henry Morgan's silver buckles, we'll see about keeping you on as one of the crew," he said as he closed the door behind him and left Gemma to her work.

She had dusted and rubbed and shone until the bookcases, the windows and the chairs all gleamed.

She gave a final rub to the small globe that spun in a brass stand on Captain Thackery's desk. As she did so, she gazed out of the long leaded window that stretched along the far end of Jake's cabin. Through the hundred diamond-shaped panes of glass, she could see a long, silver streak of moonlight reflected on the dark waves. High up above the sea, in a jet-black sky, the real moon shone like one of the pearls from her necklace.

Crash! Gemma caught the tiny brass knob on top of the globe in the corner of her cloth and sent it clanking down on to the wooden floorboards. Quickly, she knelt down beside the two halves of the world which rolled open on the floor, like patterned bowls. She picked one up. It did not look broken. The thin rim around the edge of the bowl was smooth and unchipped. She picked up the other bowl, hoping that she could fit the two pieces back together and replace them in the brass stand. Then she noticed a slender tube of rolled-up paper lying beside her knee. It was a tiny scroll, tied with a red ribbon. It must have fallen out of the globe when it landed. She rested the two halves of the world on the floor, picked up the tube of paper, untied the ribbon and unravelled the scroll. On it, handwritten in black ink, were the following words:

Captaine Jake Thackery, of the Vessel The Sea Princesse, is Commissioned to Harasse Any and Various Spanish Ships and Ports and Impounde any Spanishe Treasure discovered therein. He is hereby formally Excused from all Penalties and Punishmentes for Suche Piratical Activities against Spanishe Subjects.

At the bottom was a mark made in red, and the words 'Governor of Turtle Island'.

No wonder this piece of paper was hidden away so carefully. Spouter was right. Jake was not a plundering pirate like the captain of the *Good Fortune;* he was a privateer, commissioned by the governor to wage a secret war on the country that had been England's enemy for so long. But the English and the Spanish were not at war now. Hadn't Spouter mentioned peace on the way to Drake's Drum? He had said that it would not last long. It certainly would not if anyone got hold of this piece of paper.

Hurriedly, she rolled the paper up again and placed it into one half of the globe. Shaking with excitement, Gemma managed to fit the two halves back together and snap the whole globe back into its brass stand. She was just placing it carefully back on Jake's desk when the cabin door swung open and in walked the captain himself, followed by Spouter.

Jake smiled as he admired the spotless cabin.

"Fine work," he said to Gemma. "Now run to the galley and fetch us our supper. Tell the cook the captain wants his dinner!"

Gemma nodded and scurried to the door. Spouter whispered as she passed,

"You'll find the galley in the bow, across the deck and down the ladder. The cook's name is Potlatch. Be sure to tell him to serve up a bowl for yourself; you must be hungry by now."

Gemma was starving. She followed the warm smell of stew across the tidy, well-scrubbed deck to the galley. She nodded to Will Halfnose and Thomas Twelve-fingers who were sitting on deck, playing cards on a huge coil of rope. Bald Peg was sitting with them, whittling away at a stick with her knife. She had tied a scarf around her bald head to keep off the night chill.

Gemma climbed nimbly down the ladder and turned around as she stepped off the final rung.

"The captain wants his dinner, and Spouter says you're to serve up a bowlful for – " She stopped in her tracks. The man who stood over a great, steaming pan, holding a dented ladle in one hand and a greasy cloth in the other, was none other than Captain Red Eye's oily companion. He smiled when he saw her, and his gold tooth glinted in the candlelight.

"Well, greetin's littl'un. We meet again," he smarmed in the same slippery voice he had used earlier in the day. "What are you doing here? Don't tell me you've been treading on another cap'n's corns?"

"I'm the new cabin girl!" said Gemma, standing her ground.

"A *girrrrl* is it?" said Potlatch, rolling his Rs menacingly. "Well, I'll be blowed! Cap'n Red Eye would have been surprised to hear it was a girrrl who dared to squash his poor old bunions."

"Is Captain Red Eye a friend of yours?" asked Gemma boldly.

"I don't see what business it is of yours," answered Potlatch. Gemma didn't reply. Potlatch was right. As the newest member of the crew, she had no right interfering in the rest of the ship's business, but it didn't stop her wondering. Gemma decided to hold her tongue for now, but she was going to keep her eyes wide open.

"The captain's dinner please, and Spouter's too, and a bowlful for me," she said briskly. She waited while Potlatch spooned out three bowlfuls of stew and loaded them on to a tray with three hunks of crusty bread. Without a word, she took the tray from him, and balancing it on one arm, slowly climbed the ladder on to the deck.

"Perhaps Gemma should eat with us, it bein' her first night on board," suggested Spouter, as Gemma swayed in through the cabin door.

"Hmmm? Yes, I suppose so," replied Jake, not looking up. He was bent over a map at his desk. Spouter took the tray from Gemma and pushed it on to a clear corner of the desk. He picked up one bowl, wiped the bottom on his sleeve, and placed it under Jake's nose. Then he took another and passed it to Gemma, along with one of the pieces of bread.

"Make yourself comfy over there," he said, pointing to the padded bench that ran in front of the long window. Gemma did as he suggested. She curled herself around her bowl, drawing her legs up beneath her. The stew tasted surprisingly good.

"Potlatch doesn't look like a cook," she said, once she had eaten half her stew.

"No," said Spouter, in between slurps.

"Do you know how he got that scar around his neck?" she asked.

"'E never speaks of it, but rumour has it that one of his shipmates tried to slit his throat." Gemma looked up, but didn't ask any more. She didn't want to hear anything that might put her off her supper.

"Well, how did he come to be your ship's cook?" she asked instead.

"Ah, now that was Spouter's fault," said Jake, finally looking up from his charts and dipping his spoon into his stew for the first time. "Potlatch is another of Spouter's waifs and strays, like you. We found him standing all alone on a sandbank, half a mile from shore. It was just a tiny island, thirty feet long and three feet wide, and the tide was on the turn. If we hadn't happened to pass, he'd have drowned for sure."

"Couldn't he just have swum back to shore?" asked Gemma.

"Swim?" laughed Spouter. "I've never

known a sailor who could swim. Who wants to flounder about in the ocean? A person could catch his death doin' that sort of thing – what with the cold an' the sharks."

"Well, how did he get there?" asked Gemma.

"He told us that his ship had sunk, but I suspect he'd been marooned," said Jake.

"Marooned?" said Gemma.

"Under pirate law," explained Spouter, "a pirate that betrays his shipmates gets marooned – left on a tiny island with nothing but a flagon of water and a gun."

"No other captain would have picked up a marooned pirate," said Jake. "No one wants a fellow on board who has a habit of betraying his shipmates. But Spouter insisted. He said we shouldn't judge the poor man until we knew for sure that he was a traitor. And Spouter is not an easy man to argue with – you've seen that for yourself." Jake smiled warmly at Spouter. Gemma finished scraping her bowl.

"Henry Flintlock told me somethin' interestin' today," said Spouter, changing the subject. "Molly Doorstop told ol' Flintlock that Cap'n Red Eye raided a Spanish ship yesterday and stole an emerald – as big as his fist, she said it was! The Emerald of Intipunku...I think that's what she called it."

"Really," said Jake thoughtfully.

"The Spaniards stole it from the Indians years ago. Suddenly the King of Spain decides 'e wants it for 'is crown, so they were taking it back to Madrid."

"As big as a fist, eh?" said Jake. "And Red Eye has it?" He put his spoon down and stared into space.

"I hope you're not thinking what I thinks you're thinking," said Spouter.

"You know," said Jake, ignoring him, "I'd quite like that emerald for myself."

"Now, now," stammered Spouter. "This is Cap'n Red Eye we're talking about."

"Exactly," said Jake. "Can you imagine the look on his face when he finds it missing? Such a big emerald!"

"He'll skin you alive and strum your hamstrings!" Spouter argued.

"And, peace or no peace, think how it

would please our Royal Majesty to possess an emerald the King of Spain had set his heart upon."

"He'll tie you to the back of a whale and use you as target practice," stuttered Spouter.

"I bet he'll be holed up in Razor Cove tonight. That's where he usually hides out after a big haul," said Jake thoughtfully.

"He's already sworn vengeance on you for raiding Calamar before him!" argued Spouter.

"Then I have nothing to lose," pointed out Jake.

"You'll never manage it – not even you! No man could get hold of that emerald, not now it's in the graspin' hands of Cap'n Red Eye!"

Suddenly the two men turned, as Gemma's voice piped up from the corner.

"Maybe no man could get hold of that emerald – but with your help, I bet a twelve-year-old girl could!"

Back in Port Calico, Captain Red Eye watched as the Englishman climbed down into his tiny dinghy and rowed away to the quayside. Then he strode to the galley hatch and called to his first mate.

"Flepper! Get up here!"

A noise like that made by a big, scrabbling rat rose out of the shadowy hole, followed by a round head, blinking in the moonlight. It spoke.

"Yes, Cap'n Red Eye?"

"The crew should be back soon. We must prepare to sail with the midnight tide – we're heading for Razor Cove. We're not staying in this thieving den tonight... not with that emerald on board."

4. Sink or Swim

Dawn crept over the edge of the ocean. The *Black Heart* was anchored in Razor Cove and only the sound of snoring sailors could be heard above the swoosh and slap of water around the ship's dark hull. Everyone on board was asleep. It had been a busy night. The crew had spent the evening in the taverns of Port Calico and had then drunkenly set sail for Razor Cove, only just catching the midnight tide. It had taken most of the night to steer the swaying boat up the jagged coast. They had rejoiced over the emerald along the way – dancing, singing and firing their blunderbusses and flintlocks into the darkness in noisy celebration.

No one saw two small skiffs appear around the craggy headland of the Razor coast. No one noticed as one of the little boats bobbed towards the rocky shore and dropped anchor in the shallows. No one watched as the smaller skiff steered its way through the gentle waves towards the *Black Heart*.

In it, Gemma was rowing for all she was worth. As she neared the towering hull of the *Black Heart*, she waved to Jake and Spouter, who were crouching in the skiff moored by the shore. She had changed out of her jeans and sweatshirt and was now wearing a long yellow dress. It was embroidered with delicate blue flowers and edged with lace and pearls. The skirt was puffed out with layer upon layer of crisp cotton petticoats. Jake had found the outfit in the hold of the *Sea Princess*, stuffed amongst the treasures he had stolen from a Spanish trader. Gemma had washed her face and pinned her hair up, doing her best to copy the style of the women she had seen on the harbour side the day before.

Her heart was hammering hard as she pulled up to the side of the *Black Heart*. She took a deep breath and began to yell.

"Help! Help!" she screamed, as loudly as she could. "Help!"

On board Red Eye's ship, the pirates began to stir.

"What's that?" asked Flepper blearily, as he lifted his head from a tar-stained pile of tarpaulin on the deck.

Two sleepy pirates were leaning over the ship's railing, peering down into the sea. "It's a girl in a boat," said one of them.

"What's she want?" asked Flepper.

"I think she wants help," said the other pirate.

"Well, let's see for ourselves," said

Captain Red Eye, appearing in the doorway of his cabin. "Fetch her up."

A few minutes later, Gemma stood nervously in Red Eye's cabin. The pirate captain sat at his table and watched her intently with his crimson eye.

"My father is a rich merchant from Cadiz. His name is Julio Inglazias," she lied. "I was captured by pirates a week ago, off the coast of Florida. They were holding me for ransom." Red Eye scratched his nose and hid a greedy smile.

"You see, my father is a very rich man," continued Gemma. "He would have paid handsomely for my safe return, but I managed to escape. If you deliver me to my father, I know he will reward you."

Red Eye rested his elbows on the table and fingered his beard thoughtfully.

"Cadiz is a long way off."

"He's not there now, he's in..." Gemma fumbled for the name of somewhere in the Caribbean and wished that she had paid more attention in geography lessons, "...Cuba." She bit her lip and hoped that

Red Eye would not ask her to be more exact.

She was in luck. Red Eye was not interested in the details. As soon as he had heard the words 'rich', 'ransom' and 'reward', his mind had been whirring with plans and ideas. This struck him as the perfect opportunity to make a little easy money. An unpleasant little smirk slipped on to his lips.

"All right," he said simply.

"Really?" exclaimed Gemma incredulously. She was relieved that Red Eye had accepted her story so readily.

"You tell me where I can find your father and I'll send him a message – just to let him know you are safe and well," said Red Eye pleasantly. And how much it's going to cost him if he wants you to stay that way, he thought to himself.

Gemma opened her mouth to speak. She couldn't think of any ports in Cuba. Hurriedly, she put her hand to her forehead, and made a delicate moaning sound.

"Are you all right, my dear?" asked Red

Eye, still using his pleasant tone. After all, there was no reason to frighten this child. Not yet, anyway.

"I'm just feeling a little faint after my ordeal," said Gemma, as pathetically as she could manage.

"Of course, of course," comforted Red Eye. He stood up. "You rest here in my cabin for a while. I have things to do on deck." He smiled as sweetly as he could, which was not very sweetly at all, and left the cabin, closing the door gently behind him.

Outside, he paused for a moment. There was something familiar about this girl's face. But he was sure that he'd never seen a girl like this before, and besides, she had seemed far too pleased to see him. Most people who had met Captain Red Eye didn't look as happy if they bumped into him again. Not even a grown man would want to see Red Eye the pirate more than once in a lifetime.

Gemma didn't hesitate. As soon as she heard Red Eye's footsteps disappear, she rushed over to the big window at the end of his cabin. She opened it wide and leaned out. Slipping a small, round mirror out of her bodice, she used it to signal to Jake and Spouter waiting beside the shore. She did not know Morse code, but she let the sun glint off it a few times hoping that it would let them know that she was all right.

Then she began her search. The emerald must be in Red Eye's cabin somewhere! He wouldn't trust anyone else to take care of it.

Back on the *Sea Princess*, Potlatch was taking advantage of an empty ship. Will Halfnose, Thomas Twelvefingers and Bald Peg were ashore, replenishing the ship's fresh water supplies. The rest of the crew had gone fishing. Potlatch was the only one left on board.

Whistling happily, he strolled into Jake's cabin and began his own search. Captain Red Eye had told him to find a small scroll of paper, with the governor's signature on it. It didn't sound very interesting, but Red Eye had offered him another fifty doubloons to find it, so find it he would.

He rifled lazily through the books on Jake's desk; he rummaged through the drawers on either side; he half-heartedly flapped the maps and charts around. Slumping into the captain's chair, Potlatch leaned on the desk and puffed out his cheeks. Deep in thought, he flopped a careless hand on to the round globe which rested in a small brass stand in front of him. Listlessly, he drummed his fingers on Russia. Then he sat up. His tapping fingers made a hollow sound against the globe. Potlatch picked it up, held it close to his misshapen ear, and shook it. Something rattled inside. Maybe, just maybe, Captain Thackery was not such a wily pirate after all.

Gemma put a little more energy into her search. She rummaged and rifled at full speed, lifting and probing and opening and inspecting. She did not know what inspired her to try to unscrew the big, round, wooden knobs on the top of Red Eye's bedposts. She just thought it was strange that such a small cabin berth should have bedknobs at all.

First she tried pulling one, and when that did not work, she twisted it. Her heart lurched with excitement as the knob unscrewed in her fingers and came off in her hand. The large space inside it was empty. Gemma tried the next one. It had been screwed on more tightly than the first, which was not surprising, because inside, to her delight, Gemma discovered the huge, green, glittering emerald.

There wasn't a moment to lose. She shook the emerald out of its hiding place and scrambled across the cabin to the window. Then she heard a soft knock on the door.

"How's our little treasure feeling now?" resounded a deep voice from the hallway outside. Gemma glanced fearfully around, and swallowed hard as Captain Red Eye appeared in the doorway. It took him only a second to notice the unscrewed bedknobs and spot the stolen emerald in Gemma's hand.

"Why, you thieving squid!" he roared.

Hastily, Gemma thrust the emerald deep into her bodice. Faster than a lemming, she leaped through the open window into the sea below. She plunged into the crystal blue water and sank beneath the waves. Red Eye leaned out and peered down, trying to catch sight of her. Now he remembered that childish face! Last time he had seen it, it had belonged to a boy, a young lad in Port Calico who had trodden on his toes.

"I should have run you through there and then!" he bellowed into the ocean. "Flepper!" he yelled, turning around and heading for the deck.

Under the water, Gemma was struggling. Her long petticoats clung to her legs, wrapping tightly around them and making it impossible to kick. She flailed her arms desperately as the breath bubbled out of her mouth. It felt as though she was still sinking downwards. She could see the bright white ball of sunshine glittering through the blue water above her, but she had no idea how far up the surface was. She pulled at the water with her arms, but the weight of her dress was dragging her down. Beneath her bodice she could feel the cold, sharp edges of the emerald against her skin.

Just then, her hand scraped against something metallic. It was the rigid anchor chain of the *Black Heart*. She grasped the rusty line and began to heave herself up towards the air. It seemed like a mile to the surface, and Gemma thought her lungs would burst with the strain. She pulled and pulled, until the watery world began to blacken around the edges, and spots appeared before her eyes.

Then she bobbed, spluttering, into the light. She gasped and coughed as fresh air rushed through her. Still clinging to the chain, she wiped the hair from her eyes and the salty water from her mouth. She could hear Red Eye screaming orders up on deck. Looking up, Gemma saw him leaning, almost toppling, over the rail, scanning the water for the emerald thief.

Red Eye spotted Gemma, soaked and gasping at the stern. Still dangling over the side, he reached back and snatched a pistol from his first mate's hand. He pointed it straight at her and pulled the trigger. Nothing happened. Spitting curses, he straightened up and pushed Flepper to one side before grabbing a pistol from

another sailor. That wouldn't fire either –
it wasn't loaded. All the guns on board
were empty. Their single shots had been
fired into the black sky during last night's
celebrations, and no one had thought to
reload them.

Red Eye was now almost as purple as his
eye patch.

"Lower the skiff!" he thundered.

Down below, Gemma saw the small
wooden hull of a rowing boat appear over
the side of the ship and begin to descend
into the water. From the tattooed arms
and bandy legs sticking out over its edge,
Gemma guessed that it was crammed with
bloodthirsty pirates. She squinted into the
distance, desperately searching the shore
for Jake and Spouter, but she couldn't see
them anywhere.

The skiff, full of pirates, splashed heavily
into the sea, sending out a wave so big that
it buffeted Gemma at the far end of the
ship. Red Eye was cursing at everyone
from his position on the deck. The pirates
in the skiff lowered their oars into the
water and began to row. They started to

pull towards Gemma.

At that moment, she spotted Jake and Spouter rowing as fast as they could across the bay towards her. She tugged at her dress, but it was tangled firmly around her legs. She didn't dare let go of the anchor chain, as she could still feel the weight of her petticoats pulling her down. She couldn't get away, and even at the speed they were going, Jake and Spouter would never reach her before the pirates did.

One of Red Eye's crew suddenly stood up in the skiff.

"We're sinking!" he cried, with a look of horror on his weather-beaten face. He pointed to his feet. Gemma couldn't see it, but water was seeping fast into the boat. The crash-landing into the sea had been too much for the rotten old skiff, and enough of its planks had cracked to allow water in faster than the pirates could bail it out. Pirates can't swim, remembered Gemma with a flash of hope.

Panic broke out aboard the skiff. The crew forgot about Gemma and began scrabbling amongst themselves. The pirates on the deck of the ship started hurling empty crates and barrels over the side – anything for the struggling men below to cling to.

They were still struggling as Jake and Spouter pulled up to the stern of the *Black Heart* and hauled Gemma on board. Blind with fury, Captain Red Eye charged up and down the deck. As Red Eye fumbled hopelessly, trying to reload Flepper's flintlock with powder and lead shot, Captain Thackery pulled away with Spouter, Gemma and the Emerald of Intipunku.

5. The Tide Turns

Gemma sighed as she wriggled into her old jeans. The pretty yellow dress that had nearly drowned her still lay in a sopping heap on the floor of Jake's cabin. She had left it there while she snoozed the rest of the morning away in Jake's hammock.

There had been no one but Potlatch about when they reached the *Sea Princess* earlier. Spouter had waited for Jake and Gemma to clamber up the rope ladder on to the deck before setting off to collect Halfnose, Twelvefingers and Peg from the shore. Gemma was exhausted and had welcomed Jake's suggestion that she rest in his cabin while they sailed back to Port Calico.

Everything seemed strangely quiet after this morning's adventure, and she was feeling a little flat as she stepped out of Jake's cabin and on to the deck.

The cheer that greeted her was loud and warm. The *Sea Princess* was moored safely in the harbour at Port Calico and the crew was gathered on the deck, all clutching tankards and flagons. Jake stepped forward.

"Three cheers for Gemma, the finest pirate in the Caribbean!" The crew raised their flagons and hurrahed. Gemma thought she heard a 'yo ho ho' as well.

Pirates certainly know how to celebrate, she thought. Thomas Twelvefingers sat on a barrel with his fiddle. The melodious sound of his jigs and shanties reached right up to the crow's-nest, and the stomp, stomp, stomping of dancing pirates' boots shook the hull. Pirates dangled in the rigging and balanced on the bowsprit; they stood on the poop deck and sang, and reeled on the high forecastle. Bald Peg slapped Gemma on the back and thrust a tankard of sour ale into her hand before staggering back to join in with the dancing.

Being a pirate, thought Gemma, is every bit as good as I thought it would be. I'll have some great tips for Katie when I get home!

Just then, the door to Jake's cabin flew open with a crash that startled everyone on board and brought the music and laughter to a sudden halt. Spouter stood in the doorway with a frown on his face that would have clouded a sunny sky.

"The governor's letter…" he said slowly, as if he couldn't quite believe his own words. "It's gone. Someone's taken it!"

The crew stood in silence and looked towards their captain.

Jake, who a minute earlier had been twirling Bald Peg on his arm, stepped forward and spoke.

"This is a serious matter. The Spanish king is already furious about our raid on Calamar. He must not know that our adventure was backed by the governor himself. Spain's peace with England would be over. Have any of you seen anything that might give us a clue about where it might be?"

No one spoke. The only sound was the faint buzz from the harbour front, and the sound of the sea lapping against the boats.

"If anyone knows anything, he must speak up," said Jake urgently. "There will be no punishment, and no reward. This is a matter of honour. England's fate is at stake."

The screech of greedy seagulls fighting for food overhead shattered the nervous silence. Then an oily voice piped up from the back of the crowd.

"I think it's very suspicious that the letter should go missing the day after a new crew member comes aboard..." The weaselly voice was that of Potlatch. "The new cabin boy," Potlatch hesitated, "I'm sorry – *girrrl*," he sneered the word spitefully, "comes and goes in the cap'n's cabin as he – sorry, *she* – pleases." The other members of the crew began to turn towards Gemma as Potlatch went on.

"It seems that she's been in Cap'n Jake's cabin and the cabin of Cap'n Red Eye durin' this past day. How can we be sure which cap'n she's loyal to?" Potlatch paused, letting doubt sink into the minds of his audience.

"And don't you think it strange that Gemma should sign on to the *Sea Princess* on the very same day that Red Eye vows revenge on our good skipper?" Potlatch rubbed his hands together.

"Whose idea was it to board Red Eye's ship anyway?" he wheedled after a moment, looking Jake straight in the eye.

Jake hesitated before answering, "Gemma's..."

"Ah ha!" said Potlatch, nodding to the crew. "Perhaps I'm wrong, but maybe Red Eye sent Gemma on board this ship to steal the governor's letter. Perchance pinchin' the emerald was part of his sly plan. Perhaps it was him who told Gemma to suggest it. How do we know what went on once she was on board the *Black Heart*? Red Eye may have welcomed her with open arms, and given her the emerald in return for the letter – the letter which she had hidden in that pretty dress of hers." Potlatch raised his eyebrows questioningly, and the crew responded with gasps and nods of agreement.

"Now, now," began Jake uncertainly.

"I reckon the Emerald of Intipunku is fair payment for such a valuable slip of paper, don't you? And don't you think it's strange that a twelve-year-old girl who doesn't know her mizzen from her forecastle managed to escape from one of the most cunnin' pirates in the Caribbean?" Potlatch cajoled.

The muttering of the crew was growing

into an impatient chatter.

"I reckon Red Eye let her escape, so she could come back here and do more spyin' and thievin'!" His words had a dangerous ring of truth, especially to a crew dizzy with ale and rum. Twelvefingers put down his fiddle.

Gemma took a step backwards.

"It's not true!" she cried. Her happiness was quickly turning to fear.

"She signed the ship's articles and promised to obey pirates' law!" shouted Potlatch. "She has to pay the price for her treachery. Make her walk the plank!"

The crew cheered raucously.

"Plank's too good for her!"

"Give her Mose's Law!"

"Show her the cat!"

"Traitor!"

"Filibuster!"

Jake didn't want a mutiny on his hands. Potlatch's words had been strong and persuasive, and the crew was angry. The captain held up his hands for silence and waited. When the noise of the mob died down he said, "Fetch the plank!" Gemma gasped as Potlatch grabbed hold of her and tied her hands roughly behind her back. Will Halfnose lifted a plank from the deck. He attached it to the ship's railing so that it stuck out over the side like a deadly diving board.

"But I didn't do anything!" Gemma could hardly believe what was happening. She struggled, but her hands were fastened tightly. She couldn't reach up to unfasten her necklace and disappear back to the safety of her bedroom. She was surely going to drown this time.

Cutlass in hand, Jake stood behind her. He steered her through the boisterous rabble and on towards the plank, holding her small shoulder firmly. She wriggled as she felt his cutlass at her back. He was holding her so close now that she thought he would surely cut her arms with the sharp blade. Suddenly, Gemma twitched as the cutlass sliced through the ropes that bound her wrists.

"Don't move your arms," he breathed almost silently into her ear. "Pretend you're still a prisoner."

Jake lifted her on to the plank. He
didn't want to hurt a twelve-year-old girl,
even if she had betrayed her captain and
broken pirate law. He let go of her and

prodded her gently with his cutlass. Gemma edged to the end of the plank. It bowed under her weight. She looked down at the water far below.

Jake jumped up on to the ship's railing and stood at the head of the plank. He reached out his cutlass and hissed, "Swim under water as far as you can! I'll distract the crew. The harbour side's not far." Then he poked her softly with the tip of his sword and Gemma plummeted off the plank into the water.

Jake was as good as his word. As soon as she had disappeared under the waves, he picked up the fiddle and handed it to Twelvefingers.

"Play us up a storm! We've got a party to finish – after all, we still have the Emerald of Intipunku!" The crew cheered and rushed away from the side of the ship, eager to continue their celebrations. Only Potlatch stood at the railing, scanning the water for a sighting of Gemma.

Gemma swam as far as she could, holding her breath until her lungs felt as if they would surely burst. Then she surfaced.

There was a rowing boat moored to a small sloop nearby. She glided towards it as smoothly as she could, and ducked down behind it. She peeped towards the *Sea Princess*. The crew were dancing and singing once more, but she could see Potlatch staring out over the side. She was sure he hadn't seen her. He was looking in the wrong direction, squinting at a seagull bobbing up and down on the waves in the distance. Gemma heaved herself into the rowing boat, lay down out of sight and waited.

6. Not Quite Dry Land...

On board the *Sea Princess*, Jake sat alone in his cabin. Spouter had disappeared, muttering that he had some duties to get on with; Potlatch had asked permission to take the rowing boat ashore. On deck, the crew were sleeping off their festivities, even though it was barely tea time.

Jake leaned heavily on his desk. He stretched out his tired legs and sighed. The open globe lay in front of him. He pushed one half of it uneasily and watched it rock back and forth.

"Cap'n! Cap'n!" shouted Spouter, bursting in through the door. "I thinks I've found somethin' you'll be interested in." Spouter held out a small, dusty bag.

"I've just been lookin' in the galley. I thought it was odd Potlatch should be the one to speak out against the girl. He should know what it's like to be accused and tried on skinny evidence. I thought he should be the last to be throwin' blame at someone, bein' as he was once marooned himself. An' bein' as it was me who spoke up for Potlatch in the first place, I feels responsible. So's I went lookin' in Potlatch's bunk, and then in the galley, and here's what I found." Spouter shook some of the dust from the bag, and tipped it on to Jake's desk. Out tumbled dozens of bright, shiny doubloons.

"It seems," said Jake, "that Potlatch has a few secrets of his own. When we picked him up he was penniless, and I don't remember stealing any doubloons since he came on board. Potlatch must have a little business on the side that earned him these little beauties. Where did you find this, Spouter?"

"Hidden in a sack of grain in the galley."

"Really? Well, I think we should go ashore, find Potlatch and ask him how he came by such a large sum – and why he was so eager to keep it to himself."

Gemma had shivered in the rowing boat for what felt like hours. She wanted to be sure that Potlatch had finished his watch. As she lay there, the hot sun dried out her wet clothes and hair until only a few damp patches were left. Now she untied the knot that attached the rowing boat to the sloop's line, and lowered the oars gently into the water. Ducking down as low as she could, she sculled towards the harbour wall.

Before too long, she found herself sitting on the harbour wall, exactly where she had appeared the day before. The scene was just the same – clear blue sky, brilliant sunshine, people crowding the harbour front. Who would have thought, to see her there again, dangling her feet, that so much could have happened to this twelve year old in just one day. Gemma could hardly believe it herself. Now it felt as though her adventure was over, and that she had made an enemy of everyone she had met. She began to wonder whether she should unfasten her necklace here and now, and return to her cosy bedroom. At least she could be sure that she would never run into Red Eye or Captain Jake Thackery again. She fingered the beads at the front and began to reach around the back to unfasten the catch.

Then she noticed Potlatch, rowing away from the *Sea Princess*. Potlatch! What could he be up to now? Her hands dropped away from the necklace as she watched him rowing nearer. She stood up and wormed her way into the crowd, still keeping one eye on the treacherous pirate.

Potlatch tied his boat to one of the

harbour wall's iron rings and climbed the stone steps to the quayside. He stood still awhile, peering around, and then headed towards Henry Flintlock's workshop. As soon as he had passed, Gemma began to follow.

Potlatch made his way past the workshop, along Marlin Lane, up the steep, well-worn street towards Drake's Drum. At the top, he turned right instead of left, and pushed his way through the broken door of the Stuck Pig. Gemma hurried up to the large window at the front and peered in through a small, grubby pane of glass.

There, sitting at the best table in the centre of the bar, was Captain Red Eye. Gemma could see through the gloomy room that the pirate captain sat drumming his fingers on the battered table top. He had his back to the door, and his fancy coat was slung over the chair behind him. A shaft of sunlight radiated through the stale, dusty air and lit up his feathered hat as it lay on the table in front of him.

Gemma watched thoughtfully as Potlatch
approached and sat down beside him. He
winked, reached down, slipped two fingers
into his boot and drew out a small scroll of
paper.   The governor's letter! thought
Gemma, as Potlatch handed it to Red Eye.

Red Eye smiled greedily. He untied a small pouch from his belt and passed it to Potlatch. Then he turned in his seat and slipped the paper into the pocket of his coat.

Gemma knew that she must get that letter back. She crept to the front door of the inn. She was a different Gemma from the girl who had waited outside Drake's Drum yesterday until the crowds had cleared. Since then, she had outwitted the fiercest pirate in the Caribbean, escaped from a boatload of nasty cutthroats and walked the plank! Her palms were damp with sweat, but she didn't hesitate for a second as she stepped boldly into the roughest tavern in the whole of the West Indies.

She scanned the pirates grouped around the murky room, and walked quietly to Captain Red Eye's chair. Potlatch was counting the gold coins that Red Eye had given him, and Red Eye was leaning forward to take a swill from his tankard of ale. Carefully, silently, Gemma lifted the fancy coat from the back of the pirate captain's chair. She turned and, without looking back, strode to the door.

Stepping out into the sunshine, she ran as fast as she could down the sloping street, towards the harbour and Jake's ship. Captain Thackery would have to believe that she was not a traitor when she returned the letter safely to him. By the time she reached the bottom of the hill, she was out of breath. She stopped and panted. Then she saw Jake and Spouter rounding the corner.

Jake smiled when he saw her. Spouter gasped with surprise, delighted to see that she had survived being made to walk the plank. Gemma rushed up to them, gabbling, "I have it! The letter – it's in Red Eye's pocket...here!" Gemma held out the coat. Jake took it from her and rummaged in its deep, square pockets. He took out the letter, held it high for Spouter to see and beamed with delight.

"I..." he began, but a roar from the top of the street silenced him. Together, they turned to see Red Eye hurtling down the hill towards them, his cutlass at the ready.

"Quick," ordered Jake, "back to the ship!"

In the Stuck Pig, Potlatch was still triumphantly counting his money. He did not notice the massive, toothless, one-legged pirate who hobbled up behind him, until it was too late. Potlatch felt a large, heavy hand on his shoulder.

"Matthew Potlatch," said the one-legged pirate, in a voice as cold and mean as an arctic winter. "I never expected to see you again. Not after we'd marooned you on that tiny sand bar. You've more lives than a Spaniard's cat. And it looks like you're still up to your evil little tricks, you double-crossing sea snake." Recognising the sinister voice behind him, Potlatch turned to see the needle-sharp tip of a dagger...

Back on board the *Sea Princess*, Jake gave the order to set sail. Red Eye's ship was moored nearby. At the double, the crew hoisted the sails and hauled up the anchor. Red Eye was still clambering on board the *Black Heart* as Jake's ship steered its way out through the harbour entrance.

"We'll be at sea before his scurvy crew have unknotted their rigging and hoisted the mainsail," said Jake. "But he's sure to come after us."

7. A Fight to the Death

Jake was right. Even with a good breeze billowing the sails of the *Sea Princess*, it wasn't long before Gemma spotted Red Eye's sloop racing after them.

"Check your weapons and prepare the cannons," ordered Jake, standing at the helm. His hands steered the huge, wooden wheel in front of him. "This will be a battle to the death!"

"She's faster than we are, Cap'n, she's goin' to overhaul us," warned Spouter.

"When she draws up beside us, prepare to turn the ship. We'll fire our cannons while we're broadside and then we'll turn and ram her."

"Aye, aye, Cap'n!"

Gemma stood behind Jake on the poop deck, and stared out at Red Eye's ship as it closed in on the *Sea Princess*. It cut through the ocean at top speed.

"She's coming up on us, Cap'n," warned Spouter.

"Are the cannons primed and loaded?" asked Jake.

"Aye, Cap'n!"

"Prepare to fire!" The *Black Heart* was now almost neck and neck with the *Sea Princess*.

"Fire!" shouted Jake.

"Fire the cannons!" yelled Spouter to the crew below.

Boom! Boom! Boom! The noise startled Gemma. Smoke clouded the deck and the cannons whipped backwards, straining against their ropes as they hurled their heavy iron balls towards Red Eye's ship.

Boom! Crash! Red Eye was returning fire. There was a sound of splitting timber as a cannonball tore though the side of the *Sea Princess*'s hull. *Crack!* Another hit the foremast, splintering it. With a loud crashing and groaning, the mast toppled and smashed on to the deck. The top broke away and the sail and the crow's-nest were dragged into the sea. Ropes and splintered wood littered the deck. The helm spun out of control underneath Jake's hands, as the ship twisted in the water.

"We've lost the rudder!" bellowed Jake. *Crashunk!* Another cannonball whistled through the air and burrowed into the forecastle deck. The battered hull of the *Sea Princess* rolled slowly around until the deck was sloping gently to one side.

"Is anyone wounded?" yelled Jake, leaning slightly to keep his balance. Spouter scanned the deck where the crew were reloading the cannons.

"All hands are safe and well," he replied.

Gemma pointed towards Red Eye's ship,

"The *Black Heart* is turning – it's heading this way. It's going to ram us!"

"There's no need to ram us – we're dead in the water. Red Eye's going to board us!" said Jake.

"Check your weapons and prepare to be boarded!" Spouter shouted across the deck.

"I think you should go to my cabin, out of the way," Jake suggested to Gemma. Gemma shook her head.

"I'd rather see what's happening," she told him firmly. Jake didn't have time to argue. The *Black Heart* was turning once more and coming alongside. A shower of ropes and grappling hooks flew over the side and caught hold of the *Sea Princess*. Bald Peg was the first to hurl herself towards them, wielding a long-handled axe. Furiously, she began to slice through the lines. But more lines kept coming until the *Sea Princess* was caught hard.

Gemma could see the pirates on board the *Black Heart* now, heaving on the ropes, drawing the two ships closer and closer until their hulls touched. Captain Red Eye stood on the deck, one foot up on the capstan, holding his cutlass high in the air.

"Attack!" he screamed, bringing down his sword in a wide, swooping curve that would have sliced a man in two.

His crew began to scramble over the railings on to the deck of the *Sea Princess*. Each held a flintlock pistol in one hand, a cutlass in the other, and a dagger between his teeth. As they drew their lips away from the short, sharp blades, they seemed to smile like sea devils.

Will Halfnose let rip with his blunderbuss,

firing from the hip. A shower of shot spread across the deck, wounding two of Red Eye's crew as they approached. But the pirates kept coming, until the deck was swarming with them.

Bald Peg had thrown down her axe and pulled her cutlass out of her thick leather belt. She snarled at the ugly pirate who crept menacingly towards her. The pirate lifted his pistol, taking slow aim at Peg.

"You lily-livered mermaid's purse!" she spat, as he began to squeeze the trigger. There was a loud bang, but Peg did not stagger and fall. It was the pirate who collapsed, shot by Twelvefingers standing beside the fallen mast.

"Thanks, Thomas!" shouted Peg, and she turned and lunged towards another pirate with her cutlass.

Red Eye stepped nimbly from railing to railing and jumped down on to the deck of the Sea Princess. Gemma, still standing high up on the poop deck, saw him land. Jake was grappling with a pirate below her. She called to him as Red Eye fought his way through the scuffling pirates, but he couldn't hear through the sound of the ferocious battle. With a smart jab, Jake unbalanced his opponent. He gave him a hearty shove with his foot and sent the pirate staggering backwards down the sloping deck and crashing into a pyramid of rum casks. Jake turned just in time to see Red Eye raise his razor-sharp sword. He parried the blow with his cutlass and lunged at him with the dagger in his other hand. Red Eye returned Jake's attack with a thrust of his own dagger that sliced into Jake's arm.

Hurriedly, Gemma clambered down the steep, wooden steps from the poop deck. Red Eye and Jake parried back and forth, stepping over ropes and shattered barrels as they fought hand-to-hand. Gemma wove her way deftly through the scuffling pirates, towards the cannons. Red Eye was advancing on Jake, seething with rage and vengeance. The blood still flowed from the cut on Jake's sword arm as he struggled to fend off the fierce pirate captain.

Gemma spied an open crate strapped to

the railing beside one of the cannons. Inside lay three cannonballs, black and greasy. Gemma grasped one as best she could and heaved it out of the crate. She dumped it on the deck and held it there as she turned to locate Jake and Red Eye. She saw them on the other side of the ship, grappling face to face, until Jake thrust Red Eye away from him. Gemma let go of the cannonball. It rolled down the sloping deck towards Red Eye. She held her breath. The heavy iron ball rolled over a thick fragment of wood from the splintered mast and swerved to one side, missing Red Eye by a mile. Gemma heaved out a second cannonball, aimed it and let go. The cannonball rolled towards Red Eye once more, but a brawling pirate staggered in front of it. The ball struck the pirate on the ankle and he screamed with pain before reeling away and collapsing through an open hatch, into the hold below.

Red Eye bore down on Jake and backed him up against the remaining stump of the foremast, just as Gemma lined up the final cannonball. Red Eye, his single eye flaming with triumph, held his cutlass to Jake's throat. Powerless now, Jake let go of his sword and dagger, and they clattered to the floor. All around, the crews stopped fighting and turned to watch the two pirate captains.

"I have you now, Jake Thackery!" declared Red Eye. "I swore vengeance on you, and now I'll have it." He smiled a fiendish smile. "Say a final farewell to your crew..."

Gemma let go of the cannonball. It rolled away, down the tilting deck, straight for Red Eye.

"Cap'n!" shouted Flepper, who saw it heading towards him.

"Be quiet!" ordered Red Eye, not taking his eyes off Jake for a second. "I'm going to enjoy this."

"Cap'n!" shouted Flepper again. But it was too late. The cannonball struck Red Eye like a bowling ball striking a pin. He threw his arms out and staggered sideways. Hitting the rail at the edge of the deck, he toppled over the side with a dreadful scream, into the ocean below.

Red Eye's crew stood speechless for a moment, wondering what to do. They looked at each other doubtfully. Without Red Eye, lusting for revenge, they had no reason to murder their fellow pirates. One by one, they tucked their cutlasses away into their belts, clambered back over the railings to the *Black Heart*, and began to slice through the ropes that held the two ships together.

Flepper, alone, rushed to the side of the *Sea Princess* to search for his captain. There was no sign of Red Eye. The waves had closed over his head; the sea had swallowed him up and was not going to give him back. Flepper shook his head sorrowfully and followed his crew back on to the *Black Heart*.

Gemma looked at Jake, weary and bleeding, leaning against the broken mast. This seemed like a good time to go home. The letter was safe and Red Eye was gone. The *Sea Princess* would be in dock for a while for repairs. She picked her way across the deck to the captain's cabin.

Jake watched her go. As Gemma turned for one last look, he winked at her.

"Good shot, Gemma," he smiled, and Gemma saw the sparkle return to his dark eyes. She smiled back and stepped through the cabin door.

Inside, Potlatch's pile of doubloons still lay in a heap on Jake's desk. Gemma slipped one into her pocket – Jake won't mind, she thought, and Katie will be overjoyed to have a real doubloon! Then she undid the clasp at the back of her necklace.

Jake came striding in a moment later. He had wrapped a torn piece of sailcloth around his wounded arm. Spouter scurried in after him.

"Where's our little pirate?" asked Jake searchingly.

"Well, shiver me timbers!" said Spouter, looking around. "She's not here!"

"Shame, I was going to give her this as a reward." Jake dabbled his fingers in Potlatch's pile of gold coins, and looked thoughtful. "I reckon she must have been a sea sprite, sent by Saint Cuthbert to give us a hand." Then he smiled wickedly. "Well, I guess we'll have to keep this for ourselves. I don't think Potlatch will be back to collect it!"

The moment Gemma undid her necklace, the whole world seemed to spin around, faster and faster, and she felt as if she was falling. Then, with a bump, she landed back at her dressing table, exactly as she had been before. Smiling at her reflection in the mirror, she dropped the black and white necklace into her jewellery box. The chair felt delightfully solid beneath her, although it seemed strange not to be rolling and swaying on the ocean.

"What do you think?" A familiar voice floated in from the hall as Gemma's bedroom door opened and Katie and Mum paraded in.

"Does she look more like a pirate now?" asked Mum. Katie was still dressed in her pirate outfit, and dangling from her left ear was the golden hoop earring.

"You look great," said Gemma. "Here, I have something else for you. I found it in my jewellery box." She held out the gold doubloon that she had taken from Jake's desk. "And Mrs Bothwell is right..." She smiled a knowing smile, "Pirates do say shiver me timbers!"